Chapter One

My name is Gary Smith. I'm an ordinary sort of boy and you would expect me to have an ordinary sort of pet, wouldn't you?

No chance.

First of all, my pet is a rat. Second of all, my rat is an alien.

Honest.

He comes from another planet.

You wouldn't know to look at him but he does.

I call him Ratso – it was the first name I could think of in the circumstances.

Ratso thinks that everybody should be told who he is but I don't think it's a good idea, do you? I mean, if people got to hear about him they'd probably think the sky was full of aliens. They'd all run around building shelters, preparing for *the invasion of the killer rats from Mars* or something daft like that.

Text and illustrations copyright © Frank Rodgers 1999

First published in Great Britain in 1999
by Macdonald Young Books
an imprint of Wayland Publishers Ltd
61 Western Road
Hove
East Sussex
BN3 1JD

Find Macdonald Young Books on the internet at
http://www.myb.co.uk

Designed by Don Martin
Printed and bound by Guernsey Press

British Library Cataloguing in Publication Data available

ISBN: 0 7500 2817 3

J111,593
£8.50

My Rat is an Alien

FRANK RODGERS

MACDONALD YOUNG BOOKS

So Ratso's identity is known only to me…
and one other person.

Let me tell you how we met.

One night I was standing at the back door
gazing up at the sky. I had been playing footie
at the floodlit pitch with my pal, Bobby.

It was a lovely clear night and I was looking at the stars when suddenly I noticed that one of them was *moving*. Then, with a gasp of horror, I realized *it was coming straight towards me!* Closer and closer it rushed, looking like a tiny comet. For one horrible moment I thought it was going to hit the house.

I stood there, unable to move, my jaw dropping. But then, with a whooshing sound and a great *whump*, it shot straight into the shrubbery at the bottom of the garden instead.

My jaw had dropped so far it felt like it was on top of my trainers. I just stood and stared at the shrubbery.

Nothing moved.

I stared a bit more.

Still nothing moved.

Slowly and quietly, I turned, took the torch that was hanging by the back door and crept down the garden. To be honest I don't know why I did this. Any normal person would have run off screaming into the house, but I like mysteries and just had to find out for *myself*.

All was still when I got to the shrubbery. Very quietly I poked my torch among the leaves. Carefully I switched it on.

What I saw almost made my jaw say hello to my trainers again.

There, stuck between two branches and smoking slightly, was a strange object. It looked like three footballs stuck together and had rows of little lights winking all round it.

I had seen enough sci-fi films to know what I was looking at. It was a spaceship.

A sudden hissing noise almost made me jump out of my skin. I gulped and watched as a little hatch sprang open in the top of the first 'football'.

It was then that I felt like running. I began to back away, half expecting something nasty to leap out and grab me.

But instead of a tiny terminator, out of the hatch popped a rat.

A rat! I kid you not! A white rat with a fuzz-top hairstyle, big ears, pink eyes and a twitching nose.

I stared at the rat, wondering if it was dangerous.

The rat stared at me.

I did some more staring at the rat.

"*Chirrup whee cho cha!*" the rat called, waving its little arms around.

"Er… I'm sorry," I replied. "I don't speak Rattish."

The little creature suddenly popped back into its spaceship. It re-emerged a few seconds later and offered me a small transparent object shaped like a traffic cone.

"*Whee-prok krik,*" it said and pointed to its ear. "*Whee-prok!*"

"What is it?" I asked, taking the object carefully from its little pink fingers.

"*Krik!*" went the rat insistently and pointed to my ear this time. "*Krik!*"

I studied it closely. It was as light as a feather and didn't look dangerous so, very gingerly, I placed it in my left ear. It fitted snugly with no danger of it going in too far.

"Do you understand me now?" asked the rat.

I must admit I nearly fell over backwards.

"Wha—" I gulped. "What?"

"I said…" said the rat slowly, as if it was talking to a baby, "do… you… un… der… stand… me… now…?"

I nodded dumbly.

"Yeah," I mumbled.

"Good," said the rat briskly, climbing out of the spaceship and sitting on the edge of the hatch. "That's mighty fine, pardner. Now, tell me, who are you? A giant?"

"A giant?" I replied, surprised. "No. I'm a boy."

"A cowboy?" asked the rat eagerly.

"No… just a boy."

"So where are all the cowboys?"

"In America, I suppose," I said.

"And this isn't America?"

When I shook my head the rat banged its foot against the spaceship in annoyance.

"Gosh-durn it!" it cried. "I've done gone and crash-landed plumb in the middle of the wrong country!"

"Why are you talking like that?" I asked. "Calling me *pardner* and everything."

"I picked up a lot of westerns on my TV on the way here," said the rat. "It sure must be mighty fine to be a cowboy, yes sireee! Ridin' the range, roundin' up cattle, eatin' beans, rootin' tootin' shootin'…"

"So," I asked, "why are you here – on Earth, I mean?"

"I'm on holiday," replied the little alien.

"On holiday? Are there more of you… er… aliens here on Earth, then?"

The little alien shrugged. "I doubt it. Earth is not in any of our holiday brochures."

"So why did you come here?"

The rat smiled. "I stuck a pin in the map of the galaxy."

My mind boggled.

An alien that looked like a rat had stuck a pin in a map millions of miles away and had landed in my back garden.

An alien on holiday.

An alien who wanted to be a cowboy.

"Gosh-durn it!" he kept saying. "The wrong country! Now what in tarnation will I do?"

What will *he* do, I thought? More like what will *I* do?

I stared at the rat, my mind whirling.

The rat stared back… its mind whirling.

We just stayed there – staring at each other – our minds going round like tumble driers.

Chapter Two

"All righty, pardner," the rat said at last, "I know what I'm going to do. I'll go to the Wild West when I've fixed my spaceship. Until then I'll go sightseeing. You can show me around. Okey-dokey?"

"Well," I said slowly, wondering just how to put it, "you can't just go running around doing what you like, you know."

"Why not?" asked the rat.

"Well… because you're a rat, that's why."

"A rat? What's a rat?" asked the rat.

"*You* are," I replied. "A furry pet."

"We have pets on our planet, and let me tell you I am *not* a furry pet," cried the little creature in annoyance.

"I am a *Wheesh* from the planet *Whee*. Everyone there looks like me. My name is *Who-bro-pla-ho-preek-fro-crik.*"

"Er… Who-plo… what?"

"Listen carefully," it said and did the baby-talk routine again.

"*Who… bro… pla… ho… preek… fro… crik.* Okey-dokey?"

"Er… actually… no," I replied. "Do you mind if I just call you *Ratso*?"

"If you must," retorted the little alien huffily. "Although I don't see what's difficult about a simple name like that!"

I tried to explain about pets on Earth but Ratso found it hard to believe that everybody here would think *he* was one. He also found it hard to believe that he was tiny and that a lot of people on Earth were even bigger than I was.

"I only ever saw Earth people on TV and I just assumed they were my size," he said glumly. "Gosh-durn it, pardner. It's a bit of a shock." He folded his arms and sunk his nose on his furry chest.

Rats don't usually look cute, but at this point, Ratso did. He looked so cute and forlorn that I wanted to pick him up and tickle his little fuzzy head, but I figured he would not appreciate it. I couldn't just leave the little alien stuck in a tree so I suggested it would be better if he came inside the house.

"Okey-dokey," he said, brightening up. "We'll mosey on down to your place." He patted the side of the spaceship. "Let's go, pardner."

I knew that Ratso would have to be my secret until I had figured out what to do. Goodness knows what Mum and Dad would say if they found out I'd taken in an alien rat.

As carefully as I could, I disentangled the spaceship from the shrubbery. It was fairly light, but at the last moment it got stuck and I had to pull hard to get it free.

Ratso was still sitting on top of the open hatchway and the sudden jerk flipped him off on to the grass.

"*Yeee-ha!*" he yelled. "*Yeee-hoo!*"

Suddenly, out of the shrubbery by the fence darted two dark shapes. Before I could yell they pounced on Ratso, knocking him flat. I heard the little alien give a startled cry and my heart leapt into my mouth as I recognized the deadly next-door moggies.

Ratso lay stunned under their paws as I stumbled forward and swung the spaceship in a great arc.

"Hey!" I screamed desperately. "Get! Go on! Shoo!"

The moggies tensed, green eyes flashing and hissed at me. But the silvery *whoosh* of the spaceship unnerved them and they turned tail, disappearing over the fence with piercing howls.

I bent down and carefully picked up Ratso, my heart thumping like mad. Was he dead?

He felt just like a real rat in my hands – soft, warm and furry – and alive!

"Ring-tailed racoons and rattlesnakes!" he spluttered, shaking himself. "What were *they*?!"

I breathed a sigh of relief. "Cats," I said.

"Cats? What are cats?" asked Ratso.

"Another kind of furry pet," I explained.

"And what in tarnation were they playin' at?"

I grimaced. "They wanted to eat you," I said.

"Your pets *eat* each other on this planet?" gasped Ratso. "Gosh-durn it, pardner, that's so uncivilized! On *Whee* we're all vegetarians!"

"Er… what else do you do on *Whee?*" I asked, lifting up the spaceship.

"Do? What do you mean?" retorted Ratso.

"Well, for instance," I said, "do you go to school?"

"School? Oh yes," beamed Ratso. "I go to school every day. I'm a teacher."

I nearly dropped the spaceship.

Chapter Three

We crept upstairs past the living-room.

Mum was in there practising her karate
kicks. She had obviously just come back from
her martial arts class. I could hear her going,
"*Hai… yaa… THUMP!*" every few seconds as
she lashed out at the sofa.

Dad was in the kitchen conducting an orchestra on the radio. He is tone deaf, my dad, can't sing for toffee, but makes up for it by pretending he's a famous conductor. I could hear the rhythm of Ravel's *Bolero* thumping out – his favourite.

Good, I thought, they're both occupied,
I'll get past without being seen or heard… But
I had forgotten about the creaky fifth step.

"Gary?" Mum called. "Is that you?"

"Yeah, Mum," I called back quickly, frozen in
mid-step. "I'll be down in a minute."

Just then, the music stopped and Dad came into the hall. A tuneless whistle was on his lips but it stopped dead when he saw me.

"That's a *rat!*" he said.

He has a way of stating the obvious, my dad.

At that point Mum appeared, adjusting her headband.

She caught sight of Ratso and immediately that 'goo-goo' look she reserves for babies came over her face.

"Oh," she gurgled. "He's *soooo* cute! Where did you get him, Gary?" she said, reaching over the banister and tickling the fuzz on top of Ratso's head.

I felt Ratso jerk.

"What is she doing?" he shouted. "She called me *cute*! She tickled me! What does she think I am?!"

"Oh, listen to the little pet," cooed Mum. "He's talking to me."

"Might be a she for all you know," muttered Dad and looked at me. "What is it, Gary? Boy or a girl? Where on Earth did you get it? And aren't rats *dirty*?"

Five minutes later I was in my room with
Ratso and the spaceship. I felt limp. Mum
and Dad had grilled me like a couple of
professional spy-catchers. I had explained
that Ratso was a stray and I had found him
in the hedge – which was true, of course –
but Dad hadn't been very pleased.

"A stray rat?" he had said. "Very strange.
Why couldn't you have found a stray dog.
Now *that* would've been all right. You can
teach a dog tricks… but a rat! You might
as well try and teach tricks to a potato!"
He pointed at Ratso. "That… *thing*… will
have to go!"

Dad liked dogs but Mum wouldn't let him have one in the house. Strangely enough, though, she loved rats, and that, in the end, was why I was allowed to keep Ratso.

"We'll advertise locally that we've found a stray rat, Gary, and if no one claims him, which I hope they don't," she said with a soppy smile, tickling Ratso's tuft of fur again, "then you can keep him. But you must take him to the vet so he can be checked over."

When they asked me about the spaceship
I had to embroider the truth a little. I said it
was a model that I was helping a friend with.
They believed that.

I sat on the edge of my bed and listened.
Downstairs Ravel's *Bolero* had started up again
and cries of "*Hai… ya!*" drifted up from the
front room where Mum had resumed beating
up the sofa.

The spaceship lay on top of my chest of drawers and Ratso stood beside it… a look of disgust on his face.

"Hog-tie and brand me!" he spluttered. "Your Ma and Pa are crazy people! Your Pa wants me to be a dog and your Ma thinks I'm the cutest thing she's ever seen!"

"She thinks you're a pet, Ratso," I explained.

"Pet? Pet? There you go again!" Ratso raged. "I'm a teacher! I'm smart! I am not a pet!"

"You *are* on this planet," I sighed.

The little creature turned on his heel, climbed into his spaceship and slammed the hatch after him.

I peered through one of the tiny windows and saw him lying on his bunk, arms behind his head, eyes tightly shut.

When I tapped on the window he ignored me.

"Good night," I called softly. "Sleep well."

Ratso glowered and turned to face the wall.

Chapter Four

Next morning was a nightmare. I woke up to find that the spaceship was empty and Ratso was missing. Frantically I searched all over the house, trying not to arouse Mum's suspicions. (Dad was out.) Ratso was nowhere to be found and with mounting anxiety I went into the back garden.

With a shock I saw that the next-door moggies were there, crouched low among the bedding plants at the bottom of the garden. I just knew they were after Ratso.

I ran towards them in panic, waving my arms and shouting.

"Ratso? Where are you? Watch out! Cats!"

Suddenly the deadly duo darted forward, their claws slashing at something in the long grass.

A white object shot into the air. It was Ratso.

He caught hold of a branch in the hedge and swung there, a metre or so above the surprised cats' heads. The moggies whirled round and tensed again, ready to spring.

"Oi!" I yelled, clapping my hands desperately as I ran up to them. "Go on! Beat it! Shoo!"

For a fraction of a second the cats thought about it. I could see their tiny minds working. Jump or run? They decided to run and disappeared over the garden wall in a bristling, hissing huff of fur.

"*Yeee-ha!*" cried Ratso as I lifted him off the branch. "Those cannibalistic Earth pets didn't bargain on me being able to jump so darned high!"

"What are you doing out here?" I cried. "You nearly copped it again! Those cats are after your blood!"

"Decided to go tourin' on my own," replied Ratso. "But looks like it could be a might too dangerous. Reckon I'll stick with you from now on, pardner."

"It's a rat!" said a voice behind me and, startled, I whipped round to see Bobby, my best friend, closing the gate after him. "I thought it was a big frog or something, the way it jumped away from those cats."

My heart sank. Bobby had a way of finding out about things.

"Where did you get it?" he asked.

"It's a stray," I said and started to walk back towards the house.

"A stray rat?" said Bobby suspiciously. "Strange."

"You sound like my dad," I said then muttered, "I'm going to keep him."

Just then the back door opened and Dad came out. He held up a large plastic cage by its carrying handle.

"Borrowed this from Jack Bingham," he said. "It's for the... *thing*." I could tell that Dad really didn't like Ratso.

"I'm not going in there!" Ratso shouted suddenly. "It's a prison!" He squirmed in my grasp and it was all I could do to hold on to him.

"It's for your own good," I whispered, struggling to control him. "Believe me!"

"Noisy little thing, isn't it?" remarked Bobby cheerily. "Watch it doesn't bite you."

Dad held out the open cage and I managed to put Ratso inside and lock the door. The little creature clutched the plastic grille with his pink fingers and glowered.

"Get me outa this here jail," he said between gritted teeth. "I ain't done nothin'. I'm innocent. This is a frame-up! I demand a lawyer!"

"Don't worry, Ratso," I found myself saying. "Everything will be fine." I knew that it wouldn't bother Dad or Bobby that I was talking to a rat. Everyone talks to their pets in this country.

"Ratso?" said Bobby with a grin. "Great name. Very inventive."

"Shut up, Bobby," I hissed savagely.

"Now, young man," said Dad in his sternest voice, "I've put an advert in the *Clarion* and the paper shop, but your mum and I think you shouldn't wait for a reply. We think you should take the – *thing* – to the vet today."

"Today?" I gasped. "What for?"

Dad looked at Ratso distastefully. "You never know what kinds of germs it's got," he said. "Better to get it looked at now if it's going to spend any time in our house. But with any luck the vet will put it in quarantine."

"But, Dad…" I began, but he held up his hand.

"This morning, Gary," he said. "Ten o'clock at the vet's in Ladywell Road. I made an appointment."

I sighed as he went back into the house.

Bobby clapped me on the shoulder.

"Don't worry, Gary," he said cheerfully. "I'll go with you."

Chapter Five

There were only three other people in the vet's waiting room and all three had dogs with them.

"Ooh... a white rat," said one of the lady owners sniffily. "I hope it's safe."

I didn't say a word and neither did Ratso. He had been in a huff all the way there.

The three dog owners must have been early because the vet peered round the door at that point and announced pleasantly, "Smith… rat?"

I picked up the cage and followed the vet into the examination room. The word 'quarantine' was still going round in my head accompanied by a horrible picture of Ratso stuck in the vet's back room for six months. I fervently wished that Ratso would get the all clear.

As I put the cage down on the table I realized that Bobby had come in with me.

"Er… do you want to wait outside?" I asked.

"No," he said pleasantly.

I groaned inwardly but at the same time thought, what can go wrong? It'll be over in a couple of minutes… *I hope.*

The vet beamed at me, opened the cage and, before Ratso could utter a protest, whisked the rat out and on to the table.

"Looks a fine little specimen at first glance," he said. "How old is it?"

Ratso suddenly rose on to his hind legs and glared at the vet.

"Firstly, I am a *he*, not an *it*," he said pointedly, "and secondly, my age is one hundred and six of your Earth years. I am a fully grown *Wheesh!*"

The vet grinned at the little bristling creature.

"Got a lot to say for yourself, haven't you?"

In the blink of an eye he picked Ratso up and began to examine him.

Ratso struggled futilely as the vet checked his ears and eyes, felt his limbs and looked through his fur.

"This is undignified!" he yelled. "It's an outrage!"

The vet put him back on the table and turned away towards the sink.

"Seems healthy to me," he said.

"What is it," asked Bobby. "A boy or a girl?"

I shot Bobby a dark look, but the vet smiled over his shoulder as he washed his hands.

"Should've checked that, I suppose. Be with you in a moment." He turned away again.

Ratso began to tremble.

"Should've checked that?" he spluttered. "You mean he's going to check… look at… "

His trembling grew worse and I could see he was shaking with rage.

"Ratso," I began, "calm down. You'll—"

That's as far as I got. Ratso began to vibrate so fast that his shape became a blur. Then, all of a sudden, the vibrating stopped and Bobby and I gaped.

Ratso had changed into a monkey.

The vet turned round at that point and gasped.

"Where did that spring from? Where's the rat?"

He reached for the monkey but, with a twitch of its tail, it leapt away and landed on top of the table beside the door.

Bobby stood open-mouthed but I made a grab for it.

Too late. The monkey leaned over, pulled the door open by the handle and leapt into the waiting room.

There were two minutes of absolute chaos after that.

The dogs got loose and ran round the room after the monkey, barking excitedly. Their owners chased them and screamed at the monkey. The vet darted this way and that after the monkey but never managed to catch it. Bobby stood in the doorway with his mouth open and I dodged about avoiding everyone and wondering what to do.

Finally the dogs were brought under control and the vet cornered the monkey behind a cupboard.

Putting a glove on, the vet reached in and brought out... a white rat.

I gulped in relief and took Ratso from the puzzled vet who immediately began to look for the monkey again.

Collecting the cage, I put Ratso in it and quickly left, braving the glares of the dog owners.

"It's a defence mechanism," Ratso said as I glanced at him in disbelief on the way out. "All *Wheeshes* can change shape in times of stress."

I was still in shock when half-way along the road Bobby stopped me. He had that 'don't mess me about, tell me the truth' look in his eyes.

"Don't mess me about, Gary," he said quietly. "Tell me the truth." He pointed at Ratso. "I saw what happened back there."

My heart sank to my trainers. I knew that Bobby wasn't very good at keeping secrets but what could I do?

I begged him to keep it to himself and told him everything. He took it rather well, I thought.

So, that's how it all happened.

That's how I came to have an alien rat to take care of… and a best friend to worry about in case he couldn't resist blabbing about it. Bobby said he wouldn't tell a soul and I hope he never does… but you never know, do you?

My Rat is ...

By Frank Rodgers

An exciting new Mega Stars series

Gary's rat is no ordinary pet.
Ratso is an alien from another planet.
An alien who's crash-landed in Gary's back garden...

Catch up with Ratso in these other stories:

My Rat is a Teacher

When Ratso comes to school, Gary
is worried – particularly when Derek
'The Pain' Butane is involved...

My Rat is a Hero

Ratso stows away on a school trip to
the seaside, and Gary is furious...
at first. But when there's trouble,
Ratso saves the day...

My Rat is a Cowboy

Ratso's spaceship crash lands on a
pony farm. Now he can be a *real*
cowboy. But one alien rat can cause
havoc on a horse...

For more information about Mega Stars, please contact:
The Sales Department, Macdonald Young Books,
61 Western Road, Hove, East Sussex BN3 1JD